THIS BOOK BELONGS TO

Jason Popovci -2017-

Dear Jason, here is another book
to add to our collection.
One day I hope you can read this
book to me without my help!
I love you forever,
        Tabita ♡
   Merry Christmas!

Written by Tim Bugbird.
Illustrated by Nadine Wickenden.
Designed by Annie Simpson.

The Perfect Gift

Tim Bugbird • Nadine Wickenden

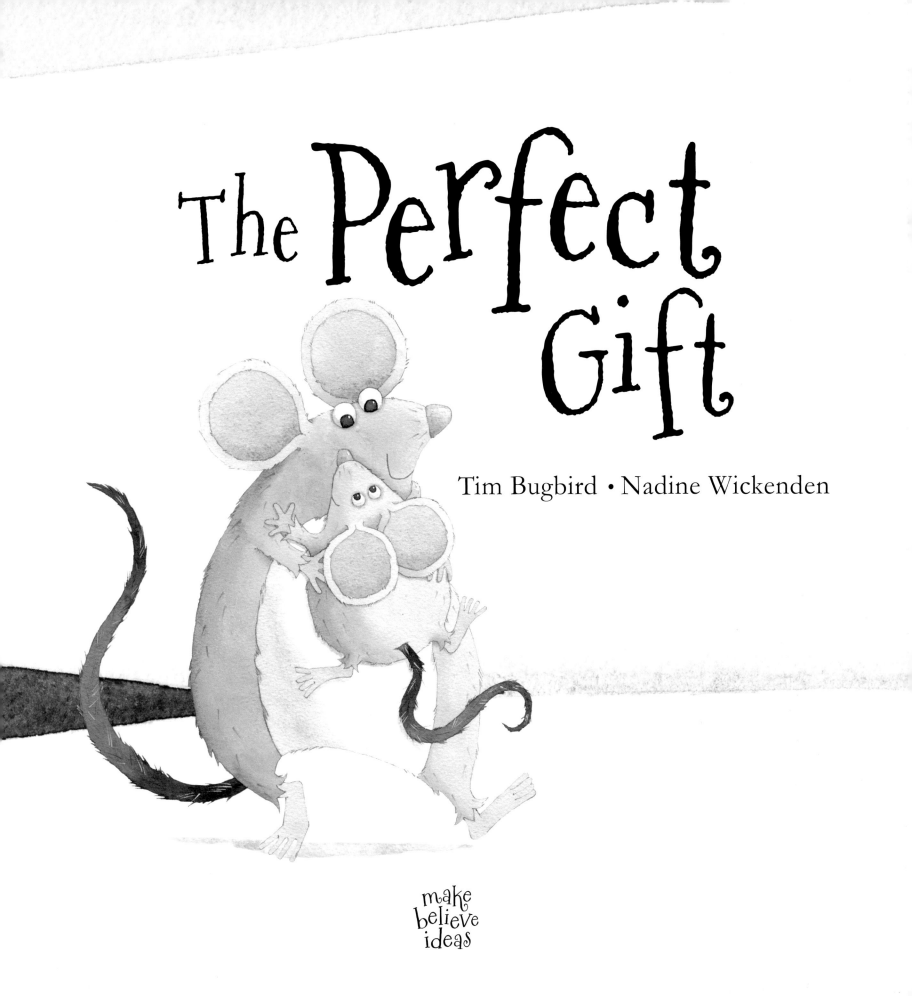

make
believe
ideas

Three days before Christmas,
Little Squeak was playing
in the forest when he
saw a beautiful acorn.
"This will be the perfect gift
for Big," he thought.

Little Squeak carefully wrapped the acorn in a **golden leaf** and hid it in the hollow of an old tree trunk.

On Christmas Eve, Little Squeak collected the acorn.

But just moments from home, it slipped from his paws,

rolled into the stream, and was washed away.

"I'm sorry," he said to Big.

"I lost your gift and have nothing

to give you for Christmas."

"But you have already given me so much!" replied Big.

"Dry your tears, and I'll explain . . ."

The gift you give has no shape or size.
It's the love that I see
when I look in
your eyes.

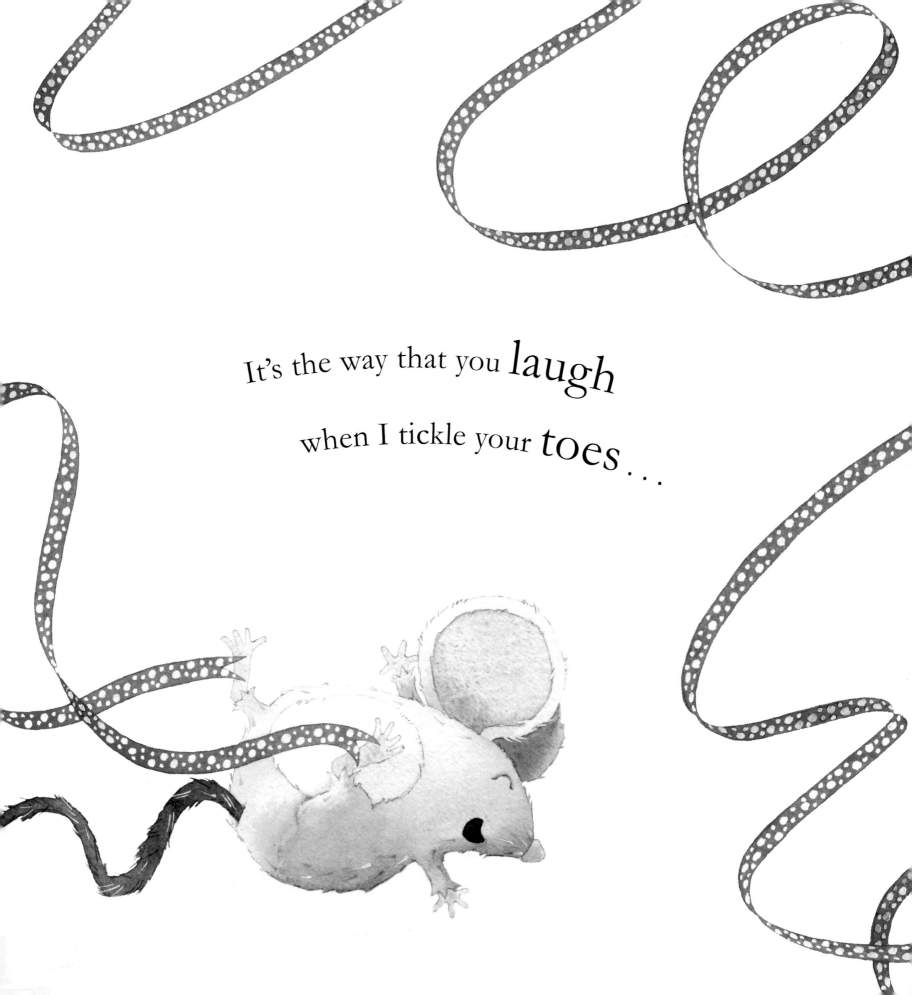

It's the way that you laugh

when I tickle your toes . . .

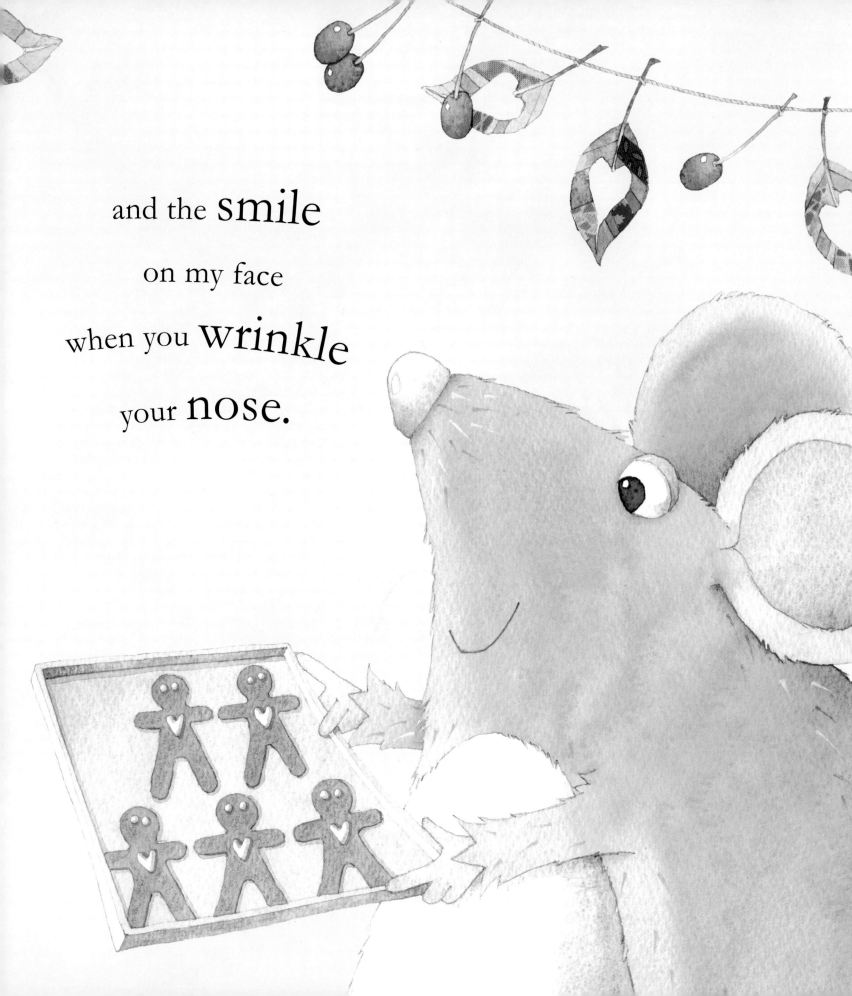

and the **smile** on my face when you **wrinkle** your **nose.**

It's not tied with **ribbons**,

and it doesn't

look **grand**.

It's the **trust** that you give

when you take my **hand**.

Your gift isn't fancy,

but inside, it glows bright.

It's the warmth

that I feel when we

cuddle up tight.

It's beautiful music – my own special sound.

It's the song in my heart

when you are around.

When there's only one left, but you say,

"This is yours,"

you give me much more

than is held in your paws.

And as time passes by, it's a gift to know

I'll receive such joy

just watching you grow.

So we'll hang up our **stockings,**

but remember what's true...

I have **all**
that I need;
the **perfect gift**
is **you!**

In the distance, a clock struck twelve; it was Christmas Day.

Little Squeak and Big looked up at the stars.
"Thank you," said Little Squeak.

"Thank **you**," said Big.

THE END